Eddie Finds A Hero

Eddie Finds

Louise Mandrell and Ace Collins

Children's Holiday Adventure Series

Volume 8

THE SUMMIT GROUP

1227 West Magnolia, Suite 500, Fort Worth, Texas 76104

© 1993 by Louise Mandrell and Ace Collins. All rights reserved.

Printed in the United States of America.

93   10   9   8   7   6   5   4   3   2   1

Jacket and Book Design by Cheryl Corbitt

LIBRARY OF CONGRESS CATALOGING-IN-PUBLICATION DATA

Mandrell, Louise.

   Eddie finds a hero / Louise Mandrell and Ace Collins; illustrated by Steve Grey.

   p. cm. – (Louise Mandrell & Ace Collins holiday adventure series; v. 8)

   Summary: Eddie, whose world is filled with baseball while his father is away fighting in World
War II, has his entire life put into new perspective by a telegram, the words of his best friend, and
a letter from his father.

   ISBN 1-56530-037-8: $12.95

   1. World War, 1939-1945 – United States – Juvenile fiction. [1. World War, 1939-1945 –
United States – Fiction. 2. Memorial Day – Fiction. 3. Baseball – Fiction.] I. Collins, Ace. II. Grey,
Steve, ill. III. Title. IV. Series: Mandrell, Louise. Louise Mandrell & Ace Collins holiday adventure
series; v. 8.

PZ7. M31254Ed   1993

[Fic] – dc20   93-300

CIP

AC

A Hero

Illustrated by Steve Grey

THE SUMMIT GROUP

ossing a rock into the air, the skinny boy took a mighty swing at it with an old, wooden Louisville Slugger bat. In a perfectly timed motion, honed by thousands of hours of practice, the wood and the rock met, and the stone went sailing over the backyard clothesline, across the alley, and into Mrs. Jacobs' victory garden. Smiling, the kid who dreamed of some day breaking Babe Ruth's home-run record cocked his St. Louis cap back on his head, tapped the ground with the finely sanded piece of ash, and began to look for something else to hit.

Everyone in the small town of Royal knew that baseball was the most important thing in Eddie Roe's life. The freckled-faced twelve-year-old lived for the game. From spring training to the World Series, it was all he thought about. During summer vacations, the only time that he wasn't out playing baseball in the hot, Illinois sun, he was camped in front of the family radio, listening to his beloved St. Louis Cardinals or their rivals, the Chicago Cubs.

Even at night, when it was too dark to play, he didn't quit thinking about balls and strikes or hits and errors. He would sit on his bed for hours, the squares of colorful cardboard spread out around him, and study his treasured baseball cards.

Eddie had been collecting baseball cards for years. He had the stars, like Bob Feller, Dizzy Dean, Jimmie Fox, Carl Hubbell, and Hank Greenberg. These were the cards that his friends all wanted. But Eddie had a favorite card. And it wasn't even of a player from his favorite team, the Cardinals. The bubble gum premium that was most important to him had been released a decade before, when Eddie was only two. There was nothing that he would trade for his ten-year-old Lou Gehrig Goudey chewing gum card.

Eddie loved the legendary Gehrig because of the way the man had played. He was in Yankee pinstripes every time there was a game. He was a man of great courage. Before a disease killed him during the prime of his life, the New York first baseman had said that he had been a lucky man just because he had been able to play the sport. Surely there could be no better hero for a little boy than baseball's "Ironman."

Early each morning, Eddie waited by the front door and then raced out into the street to get to the morning paper first. He wanted to study the league standings, and everyone else had to wait before they could look at the front page or the comics.

Eddie's father was largely responsible for his son's interest in baseball. From the time the boy was born, the elder Roe had encouraged his son's love of the game. Every evening, after Eddie's father came home from his job at the lumberyard, he played pitch and catch with the boy. On weekends they always listened to the games together. And at least once a year the two of them made the four-hour drive to St. Louis to watch the Cardinals in action at Sportsman's Park.

All that changed when the war broke out. Clay Roe had joined the Army Air Corp in early 1942. A former airmail pilot, he was now flying bombers somewhere in Europe. The only time that Eddie ever heard from his dad was in letters.

Though Eddie missed his father, he thought he missed some of baseball's great players even more. Ted Williams, Bob Feller, and a host of others were serving in various branches of the military. The war had stolen the brightest stars of the game. To Eddie, as he dreamed of one day playing in the big leagues, this seemed the greatest tragedy of all. Baseball couldn't afford to lose men like these heroes. They should have stayed home and played the game.

"Eddie," his mother's voice called out from the back porch, "lunch is on the table."

Resting the bat on his shoulder, Eddie glanced toward the sky. Clouds were building in the west, and it looked like rain might wipe out his afternoon baseball game. Eddie said a short prayer for good weather and headed inside.

"I sure hope it doesn't rain," Eddie said between bites of his sandwich. His mouth was still half-full as he added, "I wish you could have seen the one I hit this morning. It went clear over the alley and landed in Mrs. Jacobs' – "

"You didn't break another one of her windows?" his mother interrupted frantically.

"No," the boy replied sadly, "It wasn't that good a hit."

With a relieved sigh, Clara Roe looked back at her plate. At least Eddie hadn't cost her any money yet today. With the war on, and the rationing, she didn't have any to spare.

"Nelson is supposed to come over and play catch with me," the boy announced to his family.

"Isn't that the youngest James boy?" his sister Ella asked.

Eddie just nodded his head.

"His father was killed in the battle of Midway," Eddie's oldest sister, Virginia, informed them. "Remember the big memorial service we had at church?"

"You know," Eddie broke in, disregarding most of what Virginia had said, "Mr. James met Bob Feller in basic training. Can you imagine that? Of all the luck! He even got an autograph for Nelson. I wish Dad would meet a ballplayer and get him to sign something for me."

"Just be grateful you have a father," his mother scolded. "I'm sure that Nelson considers you a lot luckier than he's been. I just pray that your father doesn't get hurt."

"Yes," Eddie added, "and I hope nothing happens to Ted Williams or Bob Feller either."

When he finished his meal, Eddie excused himself and dashed to the back door. He stopped short when he noticed that a steady rain was falling. Shaking his head, he pitched his glove on a table and slowly walked back into the living room.

His youngest sister, Sarah, was listening to the radio while she played with her doll. Smiling, she stood up when she saw Eddie drag into the room and throw himself into the large, burnt-orange chair.

"Want to play dolls with me?" she asked.

"Are you kidding?" he replied, and added, "That stupid rain has ruined everything."

Ignoring both the weather and her brother's foul mood, Sarah returned to the floor and her doll. Eddie watched her for a few minutes and then turned his attention to the rain as it rhythmically tapped the window. He was feeling so sorry for himself that he didn't notice a car drive up and park on the street in front of their house. Only the sound of the doorbell snapped him out of his trance.

"I'll get it," he shouted, getting up from the chair.

Walking through an archway, he entered the two-story home's front hallway. Three short steps took him to the front entrance. The front door was open, and through the screen door Eddie could see a man in a uniform standing on the front porch.

"Western Union," the man announced as Eddie walked up. "Is your mother at home?"

Opening the screen door so that the man could step inside, Eddie shrugged his shoulders. "I don't know," he answered. "I'll check."

Passing back through the living room, he entered the kitchen. Finding Virginia washing the dishes, he asked, "Where's Mama?"

"She's at the school organizing the war bond rally. Why?"

"A guy from some union wants to see her," he explained.

"Well," the sixteen-year-old girl answered, "tell him she's not home."

Retracing his steps, Eddie informed the uniformed man that he couldn't find his mother. "Is there anything I can do?"

"I've a telegram for her," the man explained. "Would you sign for it?"

"Sure," Eddie answered, grabbing the man's small tablet.

"What was that all about?" Ella asked, coming downstairs just as the man left.

"A telegram or something for Mama," he replied. "Do you think this rain goes as far north as Chicago? If the Cubs are playing, I can listen to them on the radio."

"You and your stupid baseball," Ella observed. "You'd think there was nothing more important in life."

"Well," Eddie shot back, "what is?"

"How about the war?" Virginia asked as she came in from the kitchen. "You do remember that Daddy's fighting in it?"

"Yeah," the boy sighed, "the war has really messed up baseball. Do you know how many good players are in the army?"

"I don't care about them," Ella shook her head. "I only care about Daddy."

A knock on the back door temporarily ended the debate. Smiling, Eddie forgot his sisters and ran through the house, still clutching the telegram.

"Nelson," he yelled as he opened the back door. "The rain has messed things up. But we can go to my room and look through my cards."

"Okay," the other boy answered. "Hey, what's that in your hand?"

"A telegram," Eddie answered. "It came a few minutes ago."

"What's it say?" Nelson asked.

"Don't know," Eddie shrugged. "Come on, let's go to my room."

As the boys passed through the living room, Eddie tossed the telegram on the table. Nelson stopped, examined it for a few seconds, and then said, "Hope it's not bad news."

"What do you mean?" Virginia asked.

"That's how we found out about my father dying at Midway," Nelson explained. "I hope this doesn't have anything to do with *your* father."

The two older girls looked first at each other and then at the small envelope. Their worried expressions made Eddie stop and think. For the first time he began to realize that his father was involved in something serious. Maybe even more serious than baseball.

"You think we should open it?" he asked.

Shaking her head, Virginia replied, "No. We have to wait for Mama. It's probably just a wire from Aunt Bess in California. You know, Uncle Ira's been sick. I doubt if it has anything to do with Daddy." Her words were meant to be reassuring, but her voice sounded frightened.

For the next few minutes, all the children just stared at the telegram. The silence was broken only when little Sarah cried out, "The postman's here! I'll get it." She scrambled to her feet, dashed to the porch, grabbed two envelopes from the mailbox, and ran back into the house. "We got two letters! Who are they for?"

"If you'd learn to read, you'd know!" snapped Eddie.

"Give them to me," Virginia ordered.

She stared at the envelopes for some time, tears forming in her eyes before whispering. "They're from Daddy. One of them is to Mama; the other is for Eddie." She placed one letter beside the telegram and handed the other to Eddie.

In the past Eddie had only casually read his father's letters. After all, when the war was over, his father would come home, and then he could tell Eddie all about it in person. But now things seemed different. The telegram had frightened all of them. Walking over to the window, Eddie studied the writing on the brownish envelope. His father had addressed the letter to Mr. Edward Roe, as though he considered his son grown up.

Turning to Virginia, he asked quietly, "You don't think that anything's happened to Dad, do you?"

Lowering her head, his sister replied, "Telegrams usually mean something bad." Choking back a sob, she added, "I hope I'm wrong."

Nelson and the three girls stared at Eddie, waiting for him to open his letter.

Eddie was scared. If this were the last mail he was ever to receive from his father, he didn't know if he wanted to read it. Maybe he could just pretend that the letter and telegram never came. Then none of this would be real.

"I wish I had a letter from my father," Nelson said. "He didn't write much. Except for that baseball card, I don't have anything left to hang onto."

"He died fighting for America," Ella said. "That's something to hold onto and be proud of. He was a hero."

"I guess you're right," Nelson replied softly. "But that doesn't make losing him any easier."

"We need to hear the letter," Virginia told her brother. "I can't stand not knowing any longer."

The radio was still on in the other room, and they heard the announcer's voice come over it, saying: *"Welcome to Wrigley Field, where today the Chicago Cubs will try to keep their four-game winning streak alive. The rain has stopped; the sun is out, and it's a beautiful day for baseball . . . ."*

For the first time in his life, Eddie walked over to the radio and turned off a baseball game. Suddenly he realized that the game he loved wasn't a matter of life or death; it was just a game.

Moving over to the big, green chair, he sat down and carefully opened the envelope. Taking a deep breath, he began to read:

Dear Eddie,
Every day when we take off on our bombing runs, I find myself a little bit more scared. Still, I have a crew that is as good as the '27

Yankees. And surrounding yourself with good people is the best way to win any game.

I met Ted Williams the other day. We had flown back from a mission with just two engines and half our tail shot off, and he was in the crowd watching us bring the plane home. You should have heard the cheers. But you'll probably never forgive me. I couldn't find a pen to get his autograph.

I've learned many things during this war, but the thing that has impressed me the most is how little time we really have and how precious it is. Having your mother, your sisters, and you makes me the luckiest man in the world. I wish I had told you and your sisters more often that I loved you. And I wish I had given each of you more of my time. If I can teach you one thing, I hope that it will be to take the time to say "thank you" and "I love you" to all the people you care about. Time is really all we have to share with others, and we need to take advantage of it while we can.

Sorry about missing the autograph. Maybe next time.

> *Love,*
> *Dad*

For a few awkward seconds, silence filled the room. No one said anything or looked at anyone else. Virginia and Ella were crying, and Eddie was choking back tears.

"You know," Eddie sighed as he pulled himself from the overstuffed chair, "when Dad left for the service, I didn't even go to see him off. While you all were at the train station saying 'goodbye,' I was playing baseball. Now I'll never get the chance to tell him I love him."

"We don't know that," Virginia said. "The telegram may mean something completely different. We can't give up yet!"

Through tear-filled eyes, Eddie stared at the telegram. Suddenly he ran across the room, grabbed it off the table, and dashed out into the rain. Wadding the telegram up in a ball, he threw it as far as he could. It landed across a fence in the Irwin's yard.

"No!" Nelson called from behind him. Running to his friend's side, he said, "That's not going to change anything."

"Why didn't I go to the train station to see him off?" Eddie cried out. "Now he's gone!"

"Do you remember how you felt when Lou Gehrig died?" Nelson asked.

"Yes," Eddie replied. He remembered. It had been awful.

"But when we play ball," Nelson explained, "both of us still pretend that we're Gehrig. In our minds, he didn't die. I've come to realize that my father is still with me, too. The things he taught me, the things he told me – they're all still a part of me. Sometimes I even find myself talking to him, and I think he hears me."

"Do you think my dad knew I loved him?" Eddie asked desperately. "Do you think he knew that, much more than Bob Feller or Ted Williams, he was my hero?"

Nodding his head, Nelson walked over and picked up the telegram. Putting his arm around his friend's shoulder, he led him back inside. As the two boys sat huddled in the living room, Virginia took the wadded up envelope, smoothed it out, and announced, "I've got to read it."

Taking a deep breath, she tore the paper open and slowly read the words.

```
MRS. CLAY ROE:

YOUR HUSBAND, CAPT. CLAY ROE, WAS SHOT DURING A

BOMBING RAID OVER EUROPE. SHOWING UNPARALLELED

COURAGE HE PILOTED HIS CREW SAFELY BACK TO

ENGLAND. HE IS IN A FIELD HOSPITAL BUT WILL RE-

COVER. HE WILL BE SHIPPED BACK TO THE STATES AS

SOON AS HE CAN TRAVEL.
```

"Did you hear that?" Virginia shouted. "He's going to
be all right! Daddy's coming home!"

The three sisters hugged each other, crying with hap-
piness. Eddie closed his eyes, overwhelmed with relief
and struggling to hold back the tears.

"I'm going down to the school and give Mama the
news," Virginia announced. "Who wants to come
with me?"

The other two girls raised their hands and ran to
the closet to find umbrellas. A still-shaken Eddie shook
his head.

"Are you going to stay here and listen to the game?"
Ella asked.

"No," he responded. "I can listen to a game anytime. I want to go over to Nelson's. I never told Mrs. James just how much Mr. James meant to me. You know, Mr. James taught me how to throw a curve ball. And two years ago he took us up to see the White Sox. He was a really nice man, and I miss him.

"Then I'm going to come home and write Dad a letter. I want him to know just how much I love him. I want him to know that everything, including baseball, means more when he's here with me."

Three weeks later, Eddie's baseball team was playing for the area championship against a group of players from Oakwood. Behind Eddie's strong pitching arm, Royal was expected to win easily. But Eddie wasn't at the game. He had found something more important to do. He was waiting at the train station.

He wanted to be the first to welcome a hero back home.

Memorial Day was first
recognized on May 13, 1868,
and called Decoration Day.
General John H. Logan,
Commander in Chief of the
U.S. Armed Forces,
ordered that the graves of all
Civil War veterans be
covered with flowers on that day.
In 1873 the state of New York
was the first to recognize
the day as a holiday.
Now called Memorial Day,
it is celebrated on the last
Monday in May.